Stories from
Hans Andersen

Stories from
Hans Andersen

Retold by
Andrew Matthews

Illustrated by
Alan Snow

ORCHARD BOOKS

To Edward
A.S.
To Marilyn and Steve
A.M.

ORCHARD BOOKS
96 Leonard Street, London EC2A 4RH
Orchard Books Australia
14 Mars Road, Lane Cove, NSW 2066
ISBN 1 85213 450 X
First published in Great Britain 1993
Text © Andrew Matthews 1993
Illustrations © Alan Snow 1993
The right of Andrew Matthews to be identified as the author and
of Alan Snow as the illustrator of this work has been asserted by
them in accordance with the Copyright, Designs and Patents Act, 1988.
A CIP catalogue record for this book is available from the British Library.

Printed in Malaysia

CONTENTS

FOREWORD

I read many different versions of Hans Andersen's stories before I wrote my own. In this retelling, I have left a few things out and added a few things, too. My aim was to make the stories immediate and enjoyable for a modern audience, while staying true to the spirit of Andersen. All the stories are well-known (though not as well-known as people think) except for ''The Pig Boy'', which I included for fun.

Andrew Matthews

THE STEADFAST TIN SOLDIER

"Tin soldiers!" shouted the little boy, as he opened his birthday present.

Carefully, he took the soldiers out of their box and lined them up in a parade across the table.

There were twenty-five soldiers, wearing red and blue uniforms, standing smartly to attention with rifles leaning on their shoulders. They all looked the same—except one. He had been made last, when the tin was running out, and he only had one leg; even so, he stood as straight as the rest. This is what happened to him.

There were other toys on the table. The most spectacular was a paper castle. In front of the castle, paper trees stood on the banks of a lake made from a small mirror. In the lake, wax swans swam on top of their reflections.

It all looked lovely, and loveliest of all was a paper dancer, who stood in the castle's open door. Her dress was white, and round her shoulders was a scarf of blue ribbon. On the scarf was a sparkling sequin, as big as her face. The dancer's arms were stretched out and one of her legs was lifted up so high that the soldier couldn't see it.

"Why, she's only got one leg, like me!" he thought. "What a perfect wife she would make . . . only . . . she lives in a castle, while I have to share a box with twenty-four other soldiers. That's no place for a lady! Oh, if only I could speak to her!"

The soldier hid himself behind a music box and gazed at the dancer, who balanced on tiptoe so beautifully.

That night, the other soldiers were packed away into their box. As soon as the people of the house were in bed asleep, the toys started to chatter and play. The crayons scribbled in the colouring books, the teddy bear turned somersaults. The tin soldiers rattled their box, trying to lift the lid so they could join in. The only toys who kept still were the dancer and the soldier, who stood firm on his one leg and stared at her without blinking.

Midnight chimed, the lid of the music box flew open and out sprang a small, ugly troll.

"Tin soldier!" the troll snapped. "Keep your eyes off that dancer!"

The soldier ignored him.

"All right—just you wait until tomorrow!" said the troll.

In the morning, when the children were up, the tin soldier was put on the window sill. Maybe it was a breeze and maybe it was troll-magic, but the window blew open

and the soldier tumbled down into the street. He landed on his helmet, with his one leg in the air and his rifle stuck in a crack in the pavement. The children hurried outside, but though they almost trod on the soldier, they didn't find him.

It began to pour down with rain. Two boys scampered up the street, holding a newspaper over their heads to keep dry.

"Here's a tin soldier!" cried one. "Let's turn him into a sailor."

They made a newspaper boat, put the soldier inside and floated him off along the gutter. It was a bumpy ride, but no matter how the boat rocked and shook and twirled, the brave tin soldier stood to attention and kept his gun on his shoulder.

"I bet this is troll's work!" thought the soldier. "Where am I off to? Oh, if the dancer were with me now, I wouldn't care where I was going!"

Up popped a water rat, who lived in the drain.

"Show me your passport!" it hissed.

The soldier stayed quiet and held his rifle even tighter. The boat raced on.

"Come back!" the rat shouted. "You can't go down the drains without having your passport stamped!"

The boat plunged into the drain, where the water crashed and roared like a waterfall. The drain flowed out into a deep canal. The soldier was spun round and round, but he kept as straight as he could, even when the boat began to sink.

"I'll never see the paper dancer again!" he thought, as the water rose over his head.

Just then, everything went dark, because a big, greedy fish swallowed him up.

"It's dark and narrow in here!" thought the soldier. "But I must be brave and stand firm!"

The fish jumped and jiggled and wiggled about and then all was quiet and still. There was a sudden flash of light and a voice shouted, "The tin soldier!" The fish had been caught, sold at market and carried to a kitchen, where a cook had cut it open with a long knife. The cook picked up the soldier and went to show everybody the strange thing the fish had swallowed.

The soldier was placed on a table and—it's a funny old world!—he found himself in the same room as before! There was the little boy, there was the castle and there was the dancer, still on tiptoe. The soldier gazed at her, but said nothing.

Maybe it was naughtiness, or maybe it was the troll again, but the little boy suddenly grabbed the tin soldier and threw him into the fire. The soldier kept straight as long as he could, but he could feel that he was slowly melting.

He gazed at the dancer and she gazed back at him.

A door slammed somewhere and a draught lifted the dancer into the air. She flew straight to the soldier and stood at his side for a moment before she burst into flames and vanished.

When the fireplace was cleared out the following morning, all that was left of the dancer was her sequin, burned black.

And the soldier? He had melted down into a tiny lump of tin, shaped like a heart.

THUMBELINA

There was once a woman who wanted a small child, but didn't know where to get one. So she went to a witch for help.

"A little child?" said the witch. "That's easy. Here's a magic seed from the warm countries. Plant it in a flower pot and see what happens!"

The woman thanked the witch, paid her with a piece of silver and went home to plant the magic seed. As soon as it touched the soil, the seed grew into a tulip, whose flower opened with a pop. In the middle of the flower sat a tiny girl.

"Why, the pretty little thing is hardly as big as my thumb!" cried the woman. "I'm going to call her Thumbelina."

The woman made Thumbelina a bed from a walnut shell. Instead of going out, Thumbelina played on the kitchen table. Her favourite game was sailing across a bowl of water in a boat made from a tulip leaf. As she sailed, she sang in a high, sweet voice.

One night, an old, damp toad got in through an open

window and hopped down on to the kitchen table.

"Just the wife for my son!" the toad declared when she saw Thumbelina sleeping in her tiny bed.

The toad picked up the walnut shell and hopped out through the window into the garden. At the bottom of the garden there was a stream with muddy banks and that was where the old toad lived with her son. He was even damper and uglier than his mother. When he saw the pretty little girl asleep in the walnut shell, all he could say was, "Ribbik! Ribbik!"

"Not so loud!" whispered the old toad. "If you wake her up, she'll run away. We'll put her on a water-lily leaf in the middle of the stream so she won't be able to escape. Then we can clear out the best room for the wedding."

In the morning when she woke, Thumbelina was startled to find herself on a big green leaf in the middle of a stream. She was even more startled when the toads appeared.

"We've come to move your bed into the best room, my dear," said the old toad. "Meet your husband. I'm sure you'll both live happily ever after."

"Ribbik! Ribbik!" croaked her son.

As the toads swam back to the bank, Thumbelina cried so loudly that the fish in the stream poked their heads out of the water to ask what the matter was. When Thumbelina told them, they all agreed it was a shame for a pretty girl like her to marry an ugly toad. They bit through the stalk of Thumbelina's lily leaf and it floated away downstream.

Thumbelina drifted past fields and towns for hours, until she was spotted by a big beetle that was flying past. The beetle grabbed her round the waist and flew her up into a tree.

"You're so pretty, I'm going to have a dinner party to show you off to my friends!" the beetle declared.

But when the other beetles arrived at the party, they said unkind things about Thumbelina.

"She's *so* ugly!"

"She's only got two legs!"

"She has no feelers at all!"

The beetle who had carried off Thumbelina was so disappointed when he heard his friends talking in this way that he ended up believing them. He flew Thumbelina down to the foot of the tree.

"Off you go!" he said. "You're far too ugly to live with me!"

All that summer, Thumbelina lived alone in the wood. She ate the sweet parts of flowers and drank the morning dew, while birds sang to her from the trees. Summer turned to autumn and then winter came. Thumbelina shivered with cold. The birds who had sung to her flew away; the trees shed their leaves and the flowers shrivelled up. It snowed, and flakes landed on Thumbelina as heavily as wet blankets. She left the wood to search for a warmer place to stay.

At the edge of the wood was a field of stubble. As Thumbelina struggled across it, she stumbled into the entrance to a field mouse's home, snug and cosy underground.

"Please could you spare me some food?" begged Thumbelina. "I haven't eaten anything for two days."

"You poor child!" said the kind-hearted field mouse. "Come in and get warm! I've got plenty of food in my pantry, so you can stay all winter, so long as you keep my house tidy and sing to me. I like a good tune."

So Thumbelina kept house and sang for the field mouse and the time passed happily.

"We're going to have a visitor," the field mouse told

Thumbelina one day. "A neighbour of mine visits me quite often. He wears such a fine black velvet coat that I'm sure he's very rich. He'd make a fine husband for you, my dear! He's blind and it's a shame he can't see how pretty you are. You must sing him your loveliest songs."

The neighbour was a mole and Thumbelina didn't like him. He talked about how much he hated the sun and flowers, even though he had never seen them. When Thumbelina sang, the mole fell in love with her at once.

"Dear field mouse," he said, "perhaps you and your young friend would like to take a stroll along the new tunnel I've dug from my house to yours. There's a dead bird in it. It fell in when the weather turned cold—stupid thing!"

The mole led the way along the dark tunnel. When he came to the place where the bird lay, he pushed his nose against the ceiling and made a hole for the sun to shine through. Thumbelina saw that the bird was a swallow. She felt sorry for it.

"Birds are such nasty creatures!" said the mole.

"I couldn't agree more," said the field mouse. "Just because they can fly, they think they're better than the rest of us."

"Poor bird!" thought Thumbelina. "I wonder if you sang for me in the summer?"

When the mole and the field mouse turned their backs, Thumbelina stroked the bird's feathers. To her surprise, she felt the swallow's heart beating.

"Why, he's not dead at all!" she whispered. "The cold has made him fall into a deep sleep. If I could make him warm, he might wake up."

She said nothing to the field mouse and the mole because they hated the swallow.

The mole blocked up the hole in the ceiling and they continued to walk. That night, Thumbelina crept out with some cotton wool to cover the bird. The next night, when she went to see him again, his eyes were open. She took him water in an acorn cup and when he had drunk it, he was able to speak to her.

At last they came to the warm countries, where there were orange and lemon trees, and lovely flowers that Thumbelina had never seen before. The further on the swallow flew, the more beautiful everything became. He showed her a ruined palace beside a blue lake.

"That's where I make my nest," he said, "but I'm sure you would rather live in one of those big flowers over there."

"Oh, yes please!" cried Thumbelina.

The swallow swooped down and set Thumbelina on a leaf next to a huge white flower. And there, in the middle of the flower, was a handsome young man, no bigger than Thumbelina herself. He wore a golden crown.

"Who are you?" Thumbelina gasped.

"I'm the prince of the flower," said the young man. "Every flower in this place has a prince or princess inside it, but I've never seen a princess as pretty as you."

Thumbelina blushed as the young man took off his crown and placed it on her head.

"Will you be my wife?" he asked her.

Thumbelina said yes at once, for the young prince was far more handsome than the toad's son and the mole. She had a fine wedding, and was given many presents by the flower princes and princesses, and was happier than she had ever been in her life.

And that's a proper ending to a story!

THE FIR TREE

A little fir tree grew in the forest. It had a sunny spot all to itself, but it was surrounded by tall trees and longed to grow.

"If I were as big as the others, I could see more of the world and birds would build nests in my branches," it said to itself.

The fir tree spent so much time wishing, it didn't notice the warm, bright sunshine, or the blue sky over its head.

In winter, when everything was covered in snow, a hare often came running along and jumped over the little fir tree, which annoyed it. Two winters passed, and by the third, the fir tree had grown so high that the hare had to run around it.

"I must keep growing!" said the fir tree. "Being tall is the only thing that will make me happy."

Every spring, the woodcutters came. They chopped down the tallest trees and carried them away on wagons.

"Where are they going?" wondered the little tree.

In late spring, when the swallows returned to the forest, the little tree asked them.

"I know," said a swallow. "They're made into masts that carry the sails on big ships. I've seen them on my way across the sea."

"How grand!" sighed the little tree. "I wish I was big enough to carry sails and go travelling over the oceans."

"You should be happy with what you've got," said the swallow. "The sun smiles on you and the wind whispers in your branches."

But the little tree wasn't happy.

At Christmas, the woodcutters returned to carry off the young trees, some of them not much bigger than the little fir tree.

"Where are they going?" the tree asked some sparrows.

"Into town," the sparrows replied. "We've seen them through the windows of fine houses, covered with things that sparkle and shine, and loaded with presents. They look beautiful!"

"Why can't that happen to me?" cried the little tree. "That sounds even better than carrying sails! Why can't I do anything but stand here in the forest?"

"You should be happy with what you've got," said the sparrows.

But the little tree still wasn't happy.

All summer, the tree grew and spread out its branches; when Christmas came, it was the first to be chopped down. The tree felt the first bite of the axe in its bark and knew nothing more until it found itself lying on a cart in the middle of town. It heard a voice say:

"That's the one we want!"

Two servants in fine coats carried the tree into a wonderful room, with portraits on the walls and silk cushions on

"I'm alone again," said the tree at last. "Talking to the mice made me think about how lovely it was in the forest. It was fun to have them scuttling through my branches, listening to my story, but all that's in the past now. Next time something happens, I must remember to enjoy it."

The next thing that happened was one morning when people came to the loft. They pulled the tree out and dragged it down to a yard where the sun shone.

"Time to grow again!" said the tree; but when it stretched out its branches, it saw that they were withered and brown.

Some boys who had danced around the tree at Christmas were playing in the yard.

"Look!" one of them shouted. "The gold star's still on the top of that ugly old Christmas tree!"

He ran across and pulled the star from the tree, snapping

its branches with his boots. After he ran off, the fir tree lay in the yard, thinking of its time in the forest.

"All in the past now," it said. "If only I'd enjoyed myself while I could!"

Servants came. They cut the tree into little bits and threw it on to a bonfire. Every crackle and spark that came from the tree as it burned was a memory of a summer day or winter night in the forest, or Christmas Eve, when it had glittered with tinsel; until, at last, the tree was burnt up and its story came to an end.

THE LITTLE MATCH GIRL

It was New Year's Eve in the old city and it was almost night. A poor girl walked the cold, dark streets in her bare feet. In the morning, she had been wearing a pair of her mother's slippers, but they were too big for her. She had lost them as she crossed a road, hurrying to get out of the way of two carts. The girl's parents had filled the pockets of her apron with matches and sent her out to sell them. All day, the little girl had trudged through the city, but no one had bought any.

It began to snow, but the girl was too tired to brush the flakes from her hair. All she could think of was how cold and hungry she felt.

She rested in a doorway, trying to keep out of the wind.

"If I go home before I've sold any matches, Father will be angry and he'll beat me," she thought.

She looked at her throbbing fingers. The cold had made them blue.

"I'll strike one match," thought the girl. "Only one, to warm my hands."

She took a match and struck it on the wall beside her. As the match spluttered and burned, its flame seemed to turn into a log fire, blazing in a polished brass hearth. The little girl smiled, stretched out her hands to the fire—and the match went out. The burning logs and gleaming hearth vanished in a flurry of snowflakes.

"Just one more," the girl whispered.

When she struck the second match, its flame seemed to shine right through the wall. The little girl could see into a room where a table was laid for dinner. There were china plates and crystal glasses, and in the middle of the table a goose sizzled in a roasting tin. To the girl's delight, the goose hopped out of the tin and came waddling towards her—and then the match went out. There was nothing to see but the cold brick wall.

The girl lit another match. This time, she seemed to be sitting under a Christmas tree. Parcels hung from its branches and the whole tree was decorated with tiny lights. The little girl reached out her hands—and the match went out. The tree disappeared and the lights became the stars, twinkling in the sky.

One of the stars fell, flashing as it went.

"Grandmother told me to make a wish whenever I saw a falling star," said the little girl; but she was too cold to think of wishes.

She struck another match and saw its flame shine in the eyes of her grandmother, who stood before her.

"I thought you were dead, Grandmother!" cried the little girl. "Please don't leave me when the match goes out! Stay with me!"

Quickly, she lit the rest of the matches. They seemed to burn brighter than sunshine. As they flared up, the little girl saw her grandmother smile and felt her grandmother's arms around her, keeping her warm and safe.

In the morning, someone found the little match girl, still sitting on the doorstep with burnt matches scattered all around her. She had frozen to death in the night, but on her face was a smile as radiant as the sun that was rising above the rooftops.

THE TINDER BOX

A soldier was walking smartly down the road, with a pack on his back and a sword at his side. He was on his way home from the wars. He hadn't gone far before he met an ugly old witch, whose bottom lip hung down over her chin.

"What a handsome young soldier!" the witch declared. "I'm going to give you more money than you ever dreamed of!"

"Thanks very much!" replied the soldier.

"See that big hollow tree over there?" said the witch, pointing with a warty finger. "Climb to the top and get right down inside it. I'll tie a rope to you so I can pull you back up."

"What shall I do when I'm inside?" the soldier said.

"At the bottom of the tree, you'll find a hall lit by a hundred lamps," the witch told him. "On one side of the hall are three doors. Go through the first door and you'll see a room in which there's a big wooden chest. Sitting on the chest will be a dog with eyes as big as saucers."

"Saucers?" gulped the soldier.

"Don't worry about him!" said the witch. "Take my blue apron with you, spread it on the floor and pop the dog on top—then open the chest and grab as many copper coins as you can carry. Of course, if you'd rather have silver, then go into the second room. There's a dog there, too, with eyes as big as bus wheels!"

"I don't like the sound of that," said the soldier.

"Not to worry," said the witch, "put him on my apron and help yourself to the money in the chest. Of course, if you'd rather have gold, you must go into the third room. The dog in there is enormous—with eyes as big as roundabouts—but sit him on my apron and he'll turn as cuddly as a kitten. Then you can help yourself to gold from the chest."

"What's in it for you?" the soldier asked suspiciously.

"All I want you to do is find my granny's tinder box," said the witch. "She dropped it the last time she was down there."

"Right you are!" said the soldier. "Tie the rope round me and give me that blue apron of yours."

The soldier climbed up the outside of the tree and lowered himself down inside it with the rope. At the bottom, he found the hall and lamps and doors just as the witch had described them.

He opened the first door and saw the dog with eyes as big as saucers.

"Don't you know it's rude to stare?" said the soldier. He opened the second door—there sat the dog with eyes as big as bus wheels.

"Aye, aye!" said the soldier. "I don't like the look you're giving me!"

He opened the third door and there was the dog with eyes the size of roundabouts.

"Oh well," the soldier whispered to himself. "Nothing ventured, nothing gained!"

He spread the blue apron on the floor, lifted the dog on to it and raised the lid of the chest. There was enough gold in

it to buy every toyshop and sweetshop in the land. Quickly, the soldier filled his pack and pockets with gold and stuffed his boots as well. He put the dog back on the chest, stepped out of the room and shouted:

"Pull me up, witch!"

"Have you got the tinder box?" the witch called.

"I forgot all about it!" admitted the soldier.

He looked around until he found the tinder box lying in a corner.

The witch hauled on the rope and soon the soldier was standing on the road again.

"What's so special about this tinder box?" he asked.

"Mind your own business!" snapped the witch. "You've

got your gold, now hand over the box before I cast a spell and turn you into a tadpole! In fact, I think I'll turn you into a tadpole anyway!"

"No fear!" cried the soldier.

He drew his sword and cut off the witch's head. Then he tied all his gold up in the apron, slipped the tinder box into his pocket and marched to the nearest town.

He took rooms in the finest inn, ordered his favourite food and bought himself smart new clothes. Because he was a rich gentleman he soon became well-known and the townspeople told him all the latest news about the cruel king and queen and the beautiful young princess who was so good.

"I wouldn't mind seeing her!" said the soldier.

"Impossible!" came the reply. "It was predicted that she would marry a common soldier and the king won't stand for it. He keeps her locked in a copper castle behind high walls."

What with throwing parties for his new, rich friends and giving money away to the poor, the soldier found his supply of gold was soon used up. He went to live in a single room in the poor part of town where none of his new friends visited him. His fine clothes became tattered.

One dark evening when he was too poor to buy himself a candle, the soldier remembered the tinder box he had found inside the tree.

"I'm sure there's a stub of candle in it!" he thought.

He found the box and struck a bright spark off its flint. At once, the door flew open and there stood the dog with eyes like saucers, saying:

"How can I help you, master?"

"Knock me sideways, the box is magic!" muttered the soldier. To the dog, he said, "Fetch me some money, would you?"

The dog ran off and came back so fast he almost bumped into himself. In his mouth was a large bag of copper coins.

The soldier discovered that one spark from the tinder box brought the dog from the chest of copper; two sparks brought the dog from the chest of silver; three made the dog who sat on the chest of gold appear.

Now he was rich again, the soldier moved back into expensive rooms, but though all his rich friends gathered round him, he wasn't happy. He kept on thinking about the beautiful princess who was locked away.

One night, the soldier made up his mind. He struck one spark from the tinder box and up popped the dog with eyes like saucers.

"I know it's late," said the soldier, "but I have to see the princess."

Straight away, the dog was off and back again, with the princess lying fast asleep on his back. She was so beautiful, the soldier had to give her a kiss before the dog carried her home.

Next morning at breakfast, the princess told the king and queen of the strange dream she had had about a dog and a soldier.

"I don't like the sound of that!" thought the queen.

That night, the princess's old nurse was ordered to hide in the princess's room to see whether what had happened was a dream or magic.

One kiss wasn't enough for the soldier. At midnight, he sent the dog again. When the dog carried off the princess, the old nurse followed as fast as she could. She saw him enter a large house and she drew a white cross on the door with a piece of chalk so she could find it again the next day.

"Now, I'm off home to bed!" she said.

When the dog took the princess back, he noticed the cross on the door, so he took a piece of chalk in his mouth and put a cross on every door in town. In the morning, when the king and queen and the nurse went searching with a company of troops, they couldn't tell which house was the right one.

But the queen was more than just a pretty face. The next night, she filled a silk bag with rice, tied it to the sleeping princess's back and cut a tiny hole in the bag so that the rice would run out and leave a trail.

At midnight, the dog came again, for by now the soldier was so in love with the princess that he wanted to marry her. The dog didn't notice the rice trail, and at dawn, guards came for the soldier and flung him into a dungeon.

"You'll hang for this," one of the guards told him.

A gallows was built in the palace courtyard. The king's guards forced a large crowd of people to cheer as the king and queen sat on their tall thrones. Then the soldier was brought out.

"One last request, Your Majesty!" he cried as the rope was placed around his neck. "Send a servant to my rooms to fetch my old pipe and tinder box—I fancy a final smoke."

The king couldn't refuse and the pipe and tinder box were brought in a matter of minutes.

The soldier made the box spark—first once, then twice, then three times—and suddenly all the dogs were by his side.

"Help me!" croaked the soldier. "Stop them from hanging me!"

The dogs rushed at the king and queen and the guards, grabbed them by the legs and noses and threw them so high into the air that they never came down again.

"Hurrah for the soldier!" shouted the people. "Marry the princess and be our king."

That's just what the soldier did. The princess was more than happy to marry the soldier of her dreams and the wedding celebrations went on for a week.

And the three dogs were guests of honour.

THE PRINCESS AND THE PEA

Whrn it was time for the young prince to be married, he went off to search for a wife. He was a choosy sort of prince—only a *real* princess was good enough for him! He travelled the world meeting princess after princess, but every one he met seemed to have something that was not quite right about her. So, after many months the prince returned home, feeling really miserable.

"This finding a real princess business is trickier than I thought," he told his parents.

One evening, there was a terrible storm. Thunder rumbled, lightning crackled and rain pelted down. Between peals of thunder came the sound of knocking at the palace gate and the king went to answer it.

A young woman was standing outside the palace. She looked awful. The wind had teased and tangled her hair and she was so wet that rain ran down the back of her neck all the way to her shoes, so that her feet squelched when she walked. The young woman said that she was a princess and asked if she could stay the night.

"*Her*? A *real* princess?" said the queen when she caught a

glimpse of their guest. "I'll soon see about that!"

The queen went off to the visitors' bedroom, pulled the mattress and all the sheets and blankets off the bed and put a pea at the bottom. Then she piled twenty mattresses on the pea and stacked twenty thick duvets on top of the mattresses.

The young woman spent the night on this peculiar bed, and in the morning the queen asked if she had slept well.

"No!" groaned the young woman. "The bed was so uncomfy! There was a hard lump in the middle that stuck into me so much, I didn't sleep at all. I'm covered in bruises!"

Now the queen knew for certain that the young woman was a princess, because she had felt the pea through twenty mattresses and twenty duvets.

"Only a *real* princess would have such delicate skin," the queen told her son.

"A real princess at last!" gasped the prince. "My search is over!"

And so the prince married the princess, and the pea was put on show in the Royal Museum. It's still there—unless someone has stolen it.

And that's a *real* story for you!

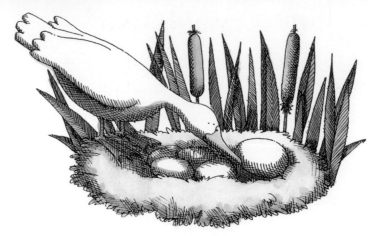

THE UGLY DUCKLING

In the shade of a clump of reeds that grew beside a pool, a duck sat on her nest, waiting for her eggs to hatch. She had grown tired of sitting there, for none of her friends had come to visit—they preferred swimming on the pond. At long last, the eggs began to crack. Yellow ducklings popped their heads out of the shells. "Peep! Peep!"

"Quack! Quick!" said the mother. "Out of those shells and into the world as fast as you like!" She peered into the nest. "Still one big egg to go. How much longer will I have to sit here?"

An old duck pushed her head through the reeds to say hello.

"How are things?" she asked.

"See my pretty ducklings?" said the mother duck. "All my eggs have hatched except this big one."

"Hmmm!" said the old duck. "It looks like a turkey's egg to me. Someone slipped a turkey's egg into my nest once, as a joke. It took a long time to hatch and the young one was useless at swimming. I'd leave it there, if I were you."

"I've hatched the others and I'll hatch this one," snapped the mother duck. "I hate leaving things half-finished."

"Please yourself," said the old duck, waddling back to the pond.

After an hour or so, the big egg cracked. The young one tumbled out. "Peep! Peep!"

"Gracious, what a big ugly duckling!" thought the mother. "He's twice the size of his brothers and sisters, and he's grey, not yellow. I wonder if he could be a turkey, like the old duck said? I'll soon find out when we go swimming."

The next morning, the sun was shining. The mother duck took her young ones to the edge of the pond. Splash!—in she went.

"Quack! Quick, follow me!" she called.

One by one, the ducklings jumped into the water—plip! plop! ploop! Before long, they were swimming happily— even the grey, ugly one.

"He's no turkey," the mother said to herself. "Look how he uses his legs! If he was a bit smaller, and more yellow, and didn't have such a long neck, he'd be quite handsome! Come with me, children! It's time you saw the farmyard. Make sure no one steps on you and watch out for the cat!"

The farmyard was busy and noisy. There were many ducks there and they stared at the newcomers in an unfriendly way.

"This place is crowded enough already!" one duck said loudly. "And we definitely don't want that big ugly duckling about the place!"

The duck flew across the yard and pecked the ugly duckling on the neck.

"Leave him alone!" said the mother. "He isn't hurting anyone!"

"He hurts my eyes with his ugly face," said the duck. "Your other children are pretty, but that grey one—ugh!"

After that, things got even worse for the ugly duckling. The ducks chased him, the hens pecked him—even his own brothers and sisters were nasty to him.

"Ugly face! Scraggy neck!" they kept saying. "We hope the cat catches you!"

At last, the ugly duckling could stand no more. He hopped over the farmyard wall and didn't stop running until he reached the muddy marshes where the wild ducks lived. There, he lay down all night, tired and miserable.

In the morning, some wild ducks flew over to look at him.

"What an ugly youngster!" sneered one. "I'm glad I don't have to look at him every day."

The ugly duckling bowed his head. He stayed on the edge of the marsh for two days, too lonely and sad to move. Then, a pair of newly hatched wild geese came across him. They were friendly and cheeky.

"You're so ugly, we feel sorry for you," they said. "Would you like to be friends and come for a swim with us? It might cheer you up."

At that moment a loud bang!—bang! split the air and the geese fell dead. There was more banging, and a huge flock of geese flew into the air. Hunters were after them. The hunters fired so many times that the smoke from their guns hung in the trees like mist. Dogs charged through the marshes, barking and splashing.

The duckling was terrified. As he was trying to hide, a great savage dog came up to him, snarling and showing its long teeth. It took one sniff and then—splosh!—it ran off.

"It must be my grey feathers!" the duckling sighed with relief. "I'm so ugly, even hungry dogs won't bite me."

The hunting went on for hours and the duckling was too frightened to move; but as soon as the shooting stopped, he ran from the marshes as fast as his little legs would go.

Just before evening, a storm gathered. A howling wind pushed and prodded the duckling. He came to a hut that was so rickety, it was only standing because the walls couldn't decide which way they should fall down. The duckling saw a hole in the door of the hut and squeezed through to find shelter.

An old woman lived in the hut with her tomcat and her hen. Next morning, the old woman noticed the ugly duckling at once, but her sight was so bad she thought he was a full-grown female duck.

"Perhaps this duck will lay me some eggs!" she said. "I'll keep it shut in for a while and see what happens."

The cat and the hen didn't like the idea of sharing their home with a stranger.

"Can you lay eggs?" asked the hen.

"No," said the duckling.

"Can you purr and catch mice?" said the cat.

"No."

"Then you'd better keep out of our way, and don't speak unless you're spoken to!"

The duckling sat down in a dingy corner. When he saw sunshine streaming through the holes in the walls, he sighed loudly.

"I wish I could be outside! I want to swim on the water and dive down to the bottom."

"What nonsense!" snorted the hen.

"It's not nonsense, it's wonderful!" the duckling cried.

"If it's so wonderful, why haven't I seen the cat or the old woman swimming about underwater?" said the hen. "You can't lay eggs, you can't purr—all you can do is sit in the corner letting your head fill up with peculiar ideas! We've taken you into our warm hut and treated you kindly, and all you do in return is talk nonsense!"

The duckling hung his head in shame.

Two children appeared on the river bank with their parents. They had come to feed the swans with bread and cake.

"Look at the new swan! Isn't he lovely!" they shouted. "See how he hides his head under his wing. He must be shy!"

The new swan did feel shy. He was used to being pecked and picked on, not admired.

"But I was such an ugly duckling!" he whispered.

"Of course you were!" laughed the other swans. "Didn't you know? Every beautiful swan was an ugly duckling once!"

When he heard this, the new swan felt full of joy and he lifted his dazzling white head to the spring sun.

THE WILD SWANS

In the land where the swallows go in winter, there lived a king who had eleven sons and one daughter, Elisa. The princes and the princess knew nothing but happiness until the day the king married again.

The new queen was beautiful, but evil. She sent Elisa away to live with poor farmers in the country and she told so many awful lies about the young princes, that the king came to hate them.

The queen cast a spell over the princes.

"Wander through the world as songless birds!" she screeched.

The princes turned into eleven wild swans. They flew out of the castle and over the great green forest that stretched as far as the sea.

Elisa knew nothing about what had happened to her brothers. She lived and worked on the farm until she was fifteen, when her father asked to see her. She was met at the

"When the waves stop rolling, I'll give up looking for my brothers, but not until then!" she said to herself.

She watched the waves. On the far horizon, the sun was beginning to dip into the sea. As the sky turned red with sunset, Elisa saw eleven white swans, crowned with gold, flying towards her. They landed beside her, and as the last of the sun slipped out of sight, the swans turned into Elisa's brothers. They hugged her, laughing and crying at the same time.

"The queen's spell only works during the day," the

oldest brother explained. "As soon as the sun sets, we lose our swan shapes. That's why we must land—if we turned back into princes while we were flying, we would fall down and be killed. We live far away across the sea, and we can only visit the country where we were born for a week in the summer, when the days are longest. This was our last day. Tomorrow, we must fly away again."

"Take me with you!" cried Elisa. "Perhaps I can find a way to break the spell."

All night, Elisa and her brothers wove a net from the branches of willow trees that grew on the banks of the stream. The net was finished just before the sun rose. Elisa was so tired that when she lay down in the net, she fell asleep at once.

The rays of the rising sun touched the princes and turned them into swans. The swans picked up the net in their beaks and flew into the sky. Though they flew as fast as they could, they only had the strength of swans and the weight of their sleeping sister slowed them down.

Elisa woke in the late afternoon. The sun was creeping down towards the horizon and there was no land in sight. Storm clouds were gathering, flashing lightning down into the waves. Elisa looked all around, knowing that if the sun set while her brothers were flying, they would turn into men and they would all fall into the sea and drown.

Half the sun was gone when Elisa saw a black rock sticking up out of the waves, looking no bigger than the head of a seal. The swans dived down to the rock and complaint. She trod the nettles with her bare feet, and when they were soft she wound them into a ball of twine.

Elisa's brothers visited her at sunset. At first, they were worried by her silence, but when they saw the strange work she was doing and the hot red blisters on her fingers and arms, they guessed that it was for them, and they left her alone.

Elisa worked all night. By the time morning came, she had finished one shirt and she started the next straight away. She had just made the first sleeve when she heard hunting horns and the barking of dogs nearby. Elisa rolled the shirt and nettles into a bundle and hid in the mouth of the cave. To her horror, a dog came leaping through the bushes. It stood outside the cave and barked at her. Other dogs followed it, and then a band of hunters appeared. The handsomest of the hunters was the king of the country. When he caught sight of Elisa, he got down from his horse and walked towards her, smiling.

"Who are you?" he asked.

Elisa shook her head and said nothing.

"This cave is no place for beauty like yours," said the king. "Come to my palace. I'll have you dressed in the finest clothes and give you delicious food to eat."

Elisa could not say no. The king lifted her up on to his horse and led her to his palace.

Elisa let serving-women bathe her. They dressed her in silk, wound strings of pearls in her hair and covered her blistered hands with a pair of satin gloves. She looked so

beautiful that when she appeared in the royal banqueting hall, all the noblemen bowed low—except the archbishop.

"Don't be taken in by her!" he told the king. "It's my opinion that she's a witch, and she's used her beauty to cast a spell over you."

But the king paid no attention to the archbishop. He took Elisa by the hand and announced that she would be his wife. He led her through the palace and showed her every room.

Elisa stayed silent. Her face was sad—all she could think of was her brothers and her unfinished task.

The last room the king showed her was tiny. It was next door to her bedroom. In the room lay the shirt, the ball of twine and the bundle of nettles from the cave.

"I could tell they were important to you, so I had them brought here because I thought it might make you happy," said the king.

Elisa smiled at him, and kissed his hand to show how grateful she was. She loved the handsome king, who was so kind to her, but she didn't dare to tell him how she felt.

They were married by the archbishop, who scowled throughout the wedding. When Elisa was made queen, the archbishop pressed the crown so hard on to her head that it hurt, but she made no complaint.

During the day, Elisa stayed by the king's side. At night, she crept into her tiny room to weave the nettles into shirts. Before she had finished the seventh, there were no nettles left.

Quietly, Elisa left the palace. She walked in the moonlight until she came to a graveyard where many nettles grew, waving their heads in the night wind. Though their stings burned like flame, Elisa gathered as many as she could carry and took them back to her room.

One person saw her—the archbishop. He couldn't sleep

that night and he looked through his bedroom window just as Elisa was returning. The next morning, he told the king what he had seen.

"Your new wife is a witch, just as I told you!" he said. "She gathers nettles by moonlight to make magic."

"I can't believe you!" cried the king.

"Then keep a close eye on her at night," said the archbishop. "If she leaves the palace again, we'll follow her."

Days went by. Elisa had finished ten shirts, but she didn't have a single nettle left. Once more, she left the palace and walked to the graveyard. This time, the king and the archbishop were behind her. They watched her picking the nettles that grew among the headstones.

"She's a witch!" hissed the archbishop. "She must be burned at the stake!"

The king rushed forward and took Elisa in his arms.

THE PIG BOY

There was once a poor prince who wished to marry a rich king's daughter. The prince had no fine presents to give—but he had a rose tree that put out one beautiful flower every five years, and he had a nightingale that sang so sweetly it made people forget their troubles; so he sent a rose and the nightingale to the princess and hoped she would be pleased with them.

The princess was delighted when she saw the rose.

"What a lovely jewel!" she smiled.

But when she touched the rose, her smile turned to a scowl.

"Ugh, Papa!" she said to her father. "It's not a jewel at all! It's a *real* rose!"

"Tut-tut!" exclaimed the king.

At that moment, the nightingale began to sing and the princess clapped her hands with joy.

"What a clever toy!" she cried. "How does it work?"

"It's not a toy, Your Highness," explained the servant who was holding the nightingale's cage. "It's a real bird."

"Well, if that's the best the prince can do, I don't even

70

want to see him, let alone marry him!" announced the princess.

The prince wasn't the sort who gave up easily, however. He put on some ragged clothes, dirtied his face with mud and went knocking on the rich king's door.

"Good morning, Your Majesty," he said. "Is there a job I could do in your palace?"

"I've got a lot of pigs that need looking after," replied the king. "It's a dirty job, but you don't look as if you'd mind that."

So the prince was made royal Pig Boy and given a hut next to the pigsty to live in. He worked in the hut all day, and by the evening he had made a pretty pot with bells around the rim. When the pot boiled, the bells rang tunes.

The princess was out walking with all her ladies-in-waiting and when she heard the musical pot, she stopped in her tracks.

"I must have that pot at once!" she declared. "Ask the Pig Boy how much he wants for it."

One of her ladies ran into the hut, holding her nose to avoid the smell of the pigs.

"How much for your pot?" she asked.

"Ten kisses from the princess," said the Pig Boy.

When the princess heard this, she was furious.

"What a rude Pig Boy!" she said. "Ask him if he'll take the kisses from my ladies instead."

"No," answered the Pig Boy, "ten kisses from the princess or I keep the pot."

"How awful!" shuddered the princess. "But I must have what I want because I'm a princess. Stand around me, ladies, I don't want anyone to see."

The ladies stood around the princess with their skirts spread out. The Pig Boy had his kisses and the princess took the pot.

"And if you dare tell anyone how I got it, I shall send you to work in the kitchens!" the princess warned her ladies.

The Pig Boy wasn't finished yet. He made a wonderful rattle; when he whirled it round, it made a sound like orchestras playing dance music.

When the princess walked past the Pig Boy's hut, the music of the rattle made her toes tap.

"Ask him how much he wants for it," she said to one of her ladies.

"A hundred kisses from the princess," came the reply.

"He's mad!" the princess shouted. She walked off angrily, but before she had taken three steps, the sound of the rattle made her feet start dancing.

"Tell the Pig Boy he can have ten kisses from me and the other ninety from my ladies," the princess said.

"We don't want to kiss the Pig Boy! He's so muddy!" protested the ladies.

"You'll do as you're told!" shouted the princess. "I'm a princess, and I must have my own way!"

But the Pig Boy would only take kisses from the princess, so once more the ladies stood around with their skirts spread out.

"What's all that fuss and bother down by the pigsty?" the king asked himself as he stepped out on to his balcony. "Why are all those ladies-in-waiting standing about?"

He was so curious that he went outside in his slippers.

The ladies were so busy counting kisses that they didn't notice the king approaching. He crept close, stood on tiptoe and saw his only daughter kissing the Pig Boy.

"Disgraceful!" he bellowed. "This is no way for a princess to behave! Out you go, both of you!"

The princess and the Pig Boy were thrown out of the palace just as it began to pour with rain.

"I've never been so unhappy!" the princess sobbed. "Even marrying that poor prince would have been better than this!"

The Pig Boy hid behind a tree, washed the mud from his face with rainwater, threw off his rags and reappeared in his princely clothes.

"I thought I loved you," he said, "but then I found out how spoilt you are. You wouldn't marry a poor prince who sent you a rose and a nightingale, but you were willing to kiss a Pig Boy to get a worthless toy. Here's your rattle. I hope it brings you luck."

The prince returned home, leaving the princess whirling the rattle round her head as she danced and cried in the rain.

push it along. The ship's decks were lined with coloured lamps and the little mermaid could hear laughter and singing. Curious, she swam closer. A friendly wave lifted her so that she could see in through the cabin windows.

She saw many finely dressed people, and the most handsome was a young prince. It was his sixteenth birthday and everybody was celebrating. The sailors danced on the deck, and when the prince came out of his cabin to watch, hundreds of rockets were fired off into the air. They burst in fiery colours that were reflected in the sea and in the prince's eyes.

The little mermaid stared and stared at the prince. Long after the birthday party ended and the prince went back into his cabin, she waited, hoping to see him again.

At midnight, a wind blew up and filled the ship's sails. It raised huge waves and made dark clouds gather. Lightning crackled and the wind howled. The ship raced between waves as high as black mountains. The little mermaid followed, thinking that the storm was great fun. Then a great wave crashed down on the ship. It snapped the masts and tipped the ship over on its side, so that water rushed in.

As the ship sank, the little mermaid remembered that humans could not live underwater. If she did not help the handsome young prince, he would drown. Through the screeching wind and lashing waves she searched for him, dodging the heavy planks and beams that floated away from the sinking ship. A bolt of lightning lit up the sky and the sea, and the little mermaid saw the prince. He had grown so weak that he could hardly swim. His eyes closed and he began to slip under. The little mermaid caught him in her arms and kept his head above the water. She held him fast all night, and though her arms ached with his weight, she would not let him go.

The sea witch was in her garden, letting her pet eels take food from her mouth. When she caught sight of the little mermaid, the witch smiled, showing the barnacles that grew on her teeth.

"I know all about you and your prince, and I know what you want," she said. "If I make you a magic potion and you swim ashore and drink it before the sun rises, your tail will split in two and turn into legs. But it will be very painful. You'll be able to walk and dance beautifully, but it will feel as though you were treading on razors. Are you willing to suffer all this to try and win the prince's love?"

"Yes," whispered the little mermaid.

"But remember," said the witch, "once you have legs, you can never be a mermaid again. And if your precious prince should marry someone else, then the morning after he has married, your heart will break and you will turn into foam on the water."

"I understand," said the little mermaid.

"And the price of my potion is . . . your voice!" the witch cackled.

"But how can I tell the prince I love him without my voice?" pleaded the little mermaid.

"Make up your mind quickly!" snapped the witch. "Time is growing short!"

The little mermaid nodded her agreement. The sea witch put her hand over the mermaid's mouth and pulled out her voice by magic; then she brewed the magic potion in a black cauldron. When it was ready, she poured the potion into a tiny bottle and gave it to the little mermaid.

"You'd better hurry," said the witch. "In the world above, the sky is already getting light."

The little mermaid swam to the surface as fast as she could. By the time she reached the prince's palace, the edge of the sun was showing above the horizon. She dragged herself on to the bottom of the marble staircase and drank the witch's potion. It burned her throat; she felt as though a sword were cutting her in half and the pain made her faint.

She woke when the sun shone over the sea, and there was the prince, standing at the top of the stairs, gazing at her in amazement. She blushed and looked down—and saw two pretty white legs where her tail had been.

The prince asked who she was and where she was from, but the little mermaid had no voice to answer him. She could only gaze at him sadly with her deep blue eyes. He took her hand and led her to the palace, and though every step felt as though she were walking on needles and knives, she walked gracefully and smiled whenever the prince looked at her.

Inside the palace, the mermaid was dressed in a silk gown. The prince's parents declared that she was the greatest beauty in the palace and insisted that she must live with them as long as she liked.

At dinner that evening, when the royal musicians played, the little mermaid rose from her place and danced. Sharp pains darted through her feet, but she ignored them, moving as lightly as a feather in the breeze. She stared at the prince, trying to tell him with her eyes and her dance how much she loved him. Though her dancing pleased him, he did not guess what it meant.

As the days went by, the prince seemed to grow more and more fond of the silent stranger he had found and the little mermaid's heart filled with hope, until one morning, when she and the prince were walking together in the palace garden.

"My dear, I've come to love you as a friend," he sighed. "And I badly need a friend I can talk to. Tomorrow I must go on a voyage to another kingdom, to meet a beautiful princess. My parents insist that I must marry her, but how can I? You see, a few months ago I was shipwrecked. The sea washed me up near a temple and a young girl from the temple found me and saved my life. That was the only time I met her, and I don't even know her name, but I know she is the only girl I could ever love."

"He doesn't know I saved him," the little mermaid thought sadly. "He doesn't know that I was the one who carried him through the waves to the temple, where he met the girl he loves more than me."

"Don't look so sad, my friend," smiled the prince. "I want you to sail with me and cheer me up with your dancing."

It took a day and a night for the prince's ship to reach harbour. The king and queen and crowds of cheering people greeted the prince, but there was no sign of the princess.

"She must have been delayed," the king explained. "I've had her educated in a temple. It's rather a long way from here and—"

A fanfare of trumpets interrupted him. The cheering crowds parted and the princess appeared.

"Why, it's her!" cried the prince. "She's the girl from the temple who saved me when I was lying nearly dead on the shore! I can't believe it! We must be married at once!"

That afternoon, the church bells rang and the crowds cheered even more loudly as the prince and princess were married in a grand cathedral. The little mermaid, in a dress of silk and gold, stood close to the prince throughout the wedding, but she saw and heard nothing. She kept on remembering the sea witch's words—

"And if your precious prince should marry someone else, then the morning after he has married, your heart will break and you will turn into foam on the water!"

In the evening, the bride and groom set sail for the prince's home. When it grew dark, lamps were lit and the sailors danced. The little mermaid danced with them, dancing for her prince one last time, though he was too busy looking at his lovely wife to notice.

It was past midnight before the dancing ended. After everyone had gone to bed, the little mermaid stayed on deck, staring down into the dark water. She thought of her father's palace below the waves and how sad it was that she would never return there. Suddenly, she saw the heads of her sisters rise out of the sea. Their hair had been cut short.

"We gave our hair to the sea witch," they said. "In exchange, she gave us this magic knife. Take it and kill the prince, and you will not die. Your tail will grow again and you can dive down into the sea with us! Hurry, that red streak in the sky means the sun will rise soon! Kill the prince and come back to us!"

The little mermaid took the knife from her sisters and hurried to the prince's cabin; but when she opened the door and saw him lying asleep, whispering his bride's name, her heart broke. She rushed back on deck and hurled the knife far out into the waves that were blood-red with the light of dawn. The little mermaid threw herself into the sea and felt her body dissolving into foam.

"I shall turn into water," she thought. "The water will rise up into clouds and fly over the land and fall as rain. The rain will run into rivers and flow back to the sea, over and over again. Wherever my prince is, on land, or sea, or in the air, I shall be with him . . . ."

Then the foam on the water vanished, and there was nothing to be seen except the great ship riding gently through the waves, and the white sea birds circling overhead.

THE EMPEROR'S NEW CLOTHES

The emperor was mad about clothes. He changed his coat every time the palace clock struck the hour, his shoes every half hour and his hat every ten minutes. In fact, the emperor was so busy dressing up in splendid outfits that he had no time for anything else.

"Fashions keep changing," he informed his prime minister, "and I must change to keep up with them."

One day, two strangers arrived at the palace. They said they were weavers with important news for the emperor, but they were really a pair of swindlers. When they met the emperor, they nudged one another and sniggered.

"Is something funny?" the emperor asked sternly.

"We couldn't help laughing at your clothes," the swindlers replied.

"What's wrong with my clothes?" the emperor asked anxiously.

"Out of date!" declared the swindlers. "No one wears silk shirts nowadays! And your coat might have been in fashion once, but not any more. It's lucky for you that we came along. We can weave a cloth so beautiful it will never go out of fashion. Once you're wearing a suit made from our special cloth, you'll be the envy of every fashionable person in the world!"

These words put an excited gleam in the emperor's eyes.

"Really?" he murmured.

"There are a couple of problems, though," one of the swindlers said slyly. "The cloth is very expensive for one thing, and for another—it can't be seen by people who are stupid or who aren't doing their work properly."

"Amazing!" the emperor whispered to himself. "Not only will I be the best-dressed person on earth, but I'll be able to tell which ministers are wise and which are foolish!" He smiled at the swindlers. "Weave me enough cloth for a new suit at once! Take as much gold from the treasury as you need."

The swindlers set up a loom in a corner of the palace and pretended to be hard at work, even though the loom was empty—unlike their pockets, which jingled with gold coins.

After a day or two, the emperor spoke to the prime minister.

"I want to know how the special cloth is coming on. You're a wise sort of chap, go and see for yourself, then report back to me."

The prime minister did as the emperor asked, but when he entered the room where the swindlers were working and saw the empty loom, he turned pale.

"I can't see a thing!" he said to himself. "I must be stupid! If the emperor finds out, I'll lose my job!"

"Well, prime minister?" smiled the swindlers. "What do you think of it?"

"And here is your long cloak," said the other. "If Your Majesty would take off all your clothes and stand in front of that big mirror, we shall help you to dress."

The emperor did just as the weavers said and let them move around him, making him step into the imaginary trousers and pull on the imaginary coat.

"I can hardly feel the cloth against my skin, it's so fine," said the emperor. He turned to his servants. "Hold up the edge of the cloak so that it doesn't drag on the ground," he said.

The two servants looked at the floor and frowned deeply.

"What's the matter?" asked the emperor. "Are you both too foolish to see it?"

"I've got it, Your Majesty!" cried one servant, bending down.

"So have I!" exclaimed the other.

And they both stood as though they were holding the cloak in their hands.

The swindlers left the palace faster than dragonflies, while the emperor went off on his parade. The streets were packed with people, all pretending that they were wise and could see the emperor's clothes.

"Hurrah for the emperor!" they shouted. "Hurrah for his new suit!"

And everybody cheered—except one little boy. He didn't know anything about the emperor's clothes. He had been too busy playing to hear the story, and grown-ups talked

about such boring things that he never listened to them anyway. When he saw the emperor waddling along, he blushed deep red.

"There's a man with no clothes on!" he gasped.

"Hush!" said his father. "That's the emperor."

"But why hasn't he got any clothes on?" shouted the little boy.

At the sound of his shout, the cheering stopped. Whispers began to run through the crowd.

"The boy's right!"

"The emperor isn't wearing anything!"

"The emperor's got no clothes on at all!"

The whispers reached the ears of the emperor, and he began to worry that they might be true.

"It can't be helped now," he told himself. "The parade must go on."

And he marched ahead more proudly than ever, followed at a distance by his ministers and the two servants, who went on holding up the cloak that wasn't there.

And that's the end of this story and all the stories in this book.